Tumbleweed Christmas

ALANE FERGUSON ✦ illustrated by TOM SULLY

Simon & Schuster Books for Young Readers

SIMON & SCHUSTER BOOKS FOR YOUNG READERS
An imprint of Simon & Schuster Children's Publishing Division
1230 Avenue of the Americas, New York, New York 10020
Book designed by Heather Wood. • The text for this book is set in Garamond.
The illustrations are rendered in oil paint. • Printed and bound in Hong Kong by
South China Printing Co. (1988) Ltd. 10 9 8 7 6 5 4 3 2 1 First Edition

Library of Congress Cataloging-in-Publication Data
Ferguson, Alane.
Tumbleweed Christmas • by Alane Ferguson; illustrated by Tom Sully—1st ed.
p.   cm.
Summary: Scotty hopes for a merry Christmas, but when he and his mother are
stranded while on a long drive through the desert, those hopes are nearly ruined.
ISBN 0-689-80465-2
[1. Christmas—Fiction. 2. Deserts—Fiction.] I. Sully, Tom, ill. II. Title.
PZ7.F3547Tu 1996 [E]—dc20 95-44058

To Larry Jones, who on a starry summer night told the
story of his own long-ago tumbleweed tree —A.F.

To the honest mechanics of the world —T.S.

Scotty peered out his car window at the sagebrush, rocks, and sand. He wished for the millionth time that the long drive through the desert would be over. Scotty and his mother were on their way to his grandparents' house for Christmas, where they would have turkey with chestnut dressing, a big evergreen tree filled with sparkling lights, and brightly wrapped gifts stacked high underneath the tree. He could hardly wait!

Suddenly, Scotty heard a loud *KaBoom KaBOOM KaBOOM KABOOM!*

Their car began to jump and shudder. Smoke curled from the engine.

"Oh, *no*!" Scotty cried, pointing to the smoke. His mother quickly pulled to the side of the road. When she lifted the hood, stinky gray clouds filled the air.

Waving smoke from her face, she said, "I don't think I can fix this. We'll have to wait in the car 'til help comes."

"We *can't* get stuck out here!" Scotty wailed. "Tomorrow's Christmas!"

"It'll be okay," his mother answered. But she looked worried as she reached into the glove compartment and pulled out a red flag. She tied it to the antenna.

Soon a rusty tow truck pulled up behind them.

"Dry Bean, Motel and Towing," Scotty read from the side of the truck.

"Looks like you've had a piece of bad luck," the man from the truck said. "My name is Jasper." He held out his hand for Scotty to shake. The skin on the back of the man's hand was crinkly, and the palm was as tough as a boot. "I can see I'm gonna have to tow you to the Dry Bean."

Scotty crossed his arms. Dry Bean did not sound good. Not good at all.

After they reached the Dry Bean, Jasper *ooohed* and *hurumphed* under the hood. At last he looked up and said, "I'm sorry, folks. I'm not sure how long this'll take to fix. It might take a spell." Wiping the grease from his hands, Jasper said, "I'll do my best to get you on your way. But just in case, you're always welcome to stay at the Dry Bean."

Scotty looked around him. His heart sank. Would he have to spend Christmas at the Dry Bean? The Dry Bean didn't have colored lights on the roof. The Dry Bean really did look like a Dry Bean.

"Do you have a Christmas tree here?" Scotty asked. "You can't have Christmas without a Christmas tree."

"Nope," Jasper replied. "I'm sorry, son. This far out, it's just me'n the coyotes." He scratched his head. "Truth is, I haven't had me a tree in years. I almost forgot about that part of Christmas."

Scotty blinked hard. "Well then, do you have a turkey? A turkey with chestnut stuffing?"

Jasper shook his head again. "Nope. But I just might be able to rustle up a can of Spam. I wasn't expectin' company for the holidays," Jasper said, tipping his hat back on his head. "I guess I don't pay much attention to Christmas fixin's. But I tell you what, Scotty. Why don't you come with me?"

They followed him inside, past some bright red oilcans stacked in one corner next to three rusty hubcaps, and a faded green couch. Jasper pulled a worn box from a shelf and blew a puff of dust from it. He thrust it into Scotty's hands.

"What's that?" Scotty asked.

"That's a carton of old Christmas frills. You pick out anything you want. Might cheer you up. I'll be right out there workin' if you need me." Then, to Scotty's mother, Jasper added, "The phone's in the garage if you want to call your folks."

A little bell jingled on the door as it shut behind them.

Scotty was alone. He sat on the faded green couch, his arms squeezed hard across his chest. That Jasper didn't know anything about Christmas!

The box Jasper had given him stood on the floor beside Scotty. He gave the box a little kick. Everything inside it fell out onto the floor—old, broken Christmas tree ornaments and faded, dusty Christmas cards.

Scotty picked up one of the cards. The writing inside it was as fine as a spider's web. "Bless your heart, Jasper," it said. "I'd still be stuck in that mud if it weren't for your kindness. Have a very merry Christmas."

Scotty slid down into the couch and looked at another card. On the front was a picture of Santa Claus riding a motorcycle.

"Merry Christmas, Jasper," the card said. "I'll never forget the way you helped me, man." The card was signed "Your pal, Spike."

Scotty felt his eyebrows crunch together as he opened a third card, and then a fourth, and then a fifth. Cards full of *thank yous* piled up around him like Christmas snow. It seemed that Jasper had helped a lot of people.

After he finished the last card, Scotty looked out the window.

A large tumbleweed bounced past and got stuck in a worn, wooden fence nearby. And then Scotty got an idea.

He worked while his mother talked to Jasper.

He worked while Jasper clinked and clanked beneath their car.

He worked until the red sun had almost set.

Behind him, the little bell jingled as his mother and Jasper came into the room.

"Let's go! The car's all fixed," his mother said. Then she stopped in surprise. "Oh, Scotty," she breathed. "Look what you've made!"

"Well, I'll be," Jasper added. "Well, I'll just be."

The setting sun shone through the window on Scotty's tumbleweed tree. He'd wound a tiny string of lights from the bottom all the way to the very top. He'd placed a red ball with missing pearls on one side of the tree, and a blue ball with broken sequins on the other. He'd put a green ball with stained ribbons on the bottom and a scratched-up silver ball at the top. He'd draped crinkled icicles into its lacy branches. Finally, Scotty had balanced a star with a broken tip on the very top of the tree.

"Merry Christmas, Jasper!" Scotty cried now. "Merry Christmas to the Dry Bean!"

"Why, that's the prettiest Christmas tree that ever was. There's not a fancy tree in the world that's as beautiful as that tumbleweed tree." Jasper swallowed hard.

The sky was fading when Jasper wiped the last of the dust from their windshield.

"Mom says we can stop here on the way back," Scotty told him. Suddenly he didn't want to leave. "Can you come with us, Jasper?" Scotty asked.

"Now, wouldn't that be nice," Jasper answered. "But I can't leave here. Someone might need my help, like you did. You folks go on and have a wonderful holiday. So long, Scotty."

As they drove along the straight highway, a pale star appeared in the darkening sky. Just then, a tumbleweed rolled across the road.

Scotty's mother said, "Don't worry, we'll be out of this dry old desert soon."

Scotty looked at the sagebrush, rocks, and sand stretched all around them. He smiled, and pressed his face into the glass.

The desert looked like Christmas.